THE
KING,
THE
MICE
AND THE
CHEESE

by
Eric and Nancy Gurney

The mice were after the king's best cheese.

SO...

The king brought in cats to chase the mice out of the palace. It worked. But then all those cats began making trouble.

SO...

The king brought in dogs to chase the cats out of the palace. Then the king began having troubles with the dogs.

SO...

The king brought in lions to chase the dogs away.

After this, things really got out of hand, and soon the whole palace was full of elephants.

AND SO...

Thanks to Eric and Nancy Gurney, here is a fine fantastic frolic. Here is a fast and funny fable for beginners—a book that will make beginners *want* to read and love it.

DATE DUE

NOV 2 1 1994			

THE
KING,
THE
MICE
AND THE
CHEESE

By NANCY and ERIC GURNEY

BEGINNER BOOKS A Division of Random House

To our grandson, Eric Gardner Bradlee

Once upon a time,
in a faraway country,
there lived a king.

He lived in a beautiful palace.

He had everything he liked.

He liked cheese best of all.

His cheese makers
made the best cheese
in all the land.

Everyone in the palace
could smell that cheese.

8

Everyone in the town
could smell that cheese.

Everyone in the country
could smell that cheese.
A mouse did.

He told all his friends about it.
Soon every mouse in all the land
was running to the palace.

The mice had fun living
with the king and eating his cheese.
But the king did not like this.

He called in his wise men.

"How can I get rid of these mice?"

he asked them.

The wise men thought
of a wonderful idea.

The wise men brought in cats . . .
big cats, little cats,
fat cats and thin cats.

The mice-chasing cats
did a very good job.

Soon all of the mice

were gone from the palace.

Now the cats were very happy.

They liked living with the king.

But the king was not happy.

He did not like living with cats.

The king called back his wise men.
"How can I get rid of these cats?"
he asked them.

"That's easy,"
said the wise men.
"We know just how
to get rid of them."

The wise men brought in dogs . . .

big dogs, little dogs,

white dogs and spotted dogs.

27

The cat-chasing dogs
did a very fine job.

Soon all of the cats
were gone from the palace.

Now the dogs were very happy.

They liked living with the king.

But the king was not happy.

He did not like living with dogs.

Once again the king
called in his wise men.
"Can you get rid of these dogs?"
he asked them.

"We surely can," the wise men said.

The wise men brought in lions . . .
big, big brave lions.

35

The dog-chasing lions did a great job.

They chased those dogs,

every last one of them,

out of the palace.

Now the lions were very happy.

They liked living with the king.

But the king was not happy.

He did not like living with lions.

For the fourth time
he called in his wise men.
"Again you must help me,"
begged the king.

Once again the wise men
said it would be easy.

Elephants!
The wise men brought in elephants
to chase the lions away.

The lion-chasing elephants
did a wonderful job.

Soon every last lion was gone.

The elephants were very, very happy
living with the king.
But the king was most unhappy
living with elephants.

47

How do you get rid
of elephants?" yelled the king.

"We can do it," said the wise men.

"We will do it right away."

They brought back all the mice.

The elephant-chasing mice
went right to work.

The mice chased
every elephant
out of that palace.

But now the poor king
was right back where he started!
Mice! Mice! They were everywhere!
Mice! Mice! Eating his cheese!

"What am I going to do?"
For three long days the king sat
and asked himself that question.
After three days of thinking,
he thought of the only answer.

The king called
all the mice together.

"Listen, boys,
let's make a deal,"
said the king.
"I'll learn how
to get along with you.
You'll learn how
to get along with me."

From then on, the king
shared his cheese with the mice . . .

. . . and the mice learned to eat
with very nice manners.